© 2007, Disney Enterprises, Inc.
Published by Hachette Partworks Ltd
ISBN: 978-1-906965-19-8
Date of Printing: June 2009
Printed in Singapore by Tien Wah Press

THE RESCUERS

DISNEY
HACHETTE

Dear Morningside
Orphanage,
I am in terrible trouble.
Please hurry.
HELP!
Penny

The Rescue Aid Society was having a
meeting. The Society was a band of brave
mice dedicated to helping those in danger.
The Chairman opened the meeting with
a report that caused a commotion among
the members. A message had been found
in a bottle washed up on the river bank.
Everyone read the note.

The message seemed to be from a little girl, and she needed urgent help from the Society. There was no time to waste! Who would go and rescue Penny?

"Mr. Chairman," said Bianca, a pretty white mouse, "may I take on this mission?"

"You?" cried the Chairman. "But you can't go all by yourself!" Everyone volunteered to go with Bianca.

But Bianca had already made up her mind.

"I'll take Bernard!" she declared. "We'll make a great team."

Bernard was the Society's janitor. He had always wanted to help those in need.

"Gosh, Miss Bianca!" he said. "Thanks!"

The two little mice, armed with a map, set off right away for Morningside Orphanage. It was a dark, rainy night and Bianca and Bernard splashed through the puddles.

Once they reached the orphanage, the
two rescuers found a box with Penny's
name on it. But as they were
looking through the things inside
the box, they were surprised by
an elderly cat.
   Bernard and Bianca got
ready to run away.
   "Don't worry about me,"
said the cat. "I'm too old to
chase after mice."
Bianca and Bernard were
very relieved that the cat was
friendly.

PENNY

"Sir, can you tell us what happened to Penny?" Bernard asked the cat, whose name was Rufus. "She's not here any more. She's gone away!" replied Rufus. The pair asked Rufus if he could think of anything that would help them find her.

Rufus remembered that a woman had offered Penny a lift. "But Penny didn't want to go with her," said the cat. "The lady and her partner have a pawnbroker's shop on this street."

"Miss Bianca, we must go and check this out!" said Bernard.

So the two little mice headed straight for the shop owned by the strange woman, whose name was Madame Medusa.

The rescuers crept
into the shop in time to
overhear the evil Medusa
screeching into her phone
to her partner:
"You clumsy idiot!
Can't you keep an eye on
that girl? I'm taking the
first flight out to Devil's
Bayou! Wait for me
there!"

"We have to follow her!" Bianca exclaimed.

"Quickly, get into the suitcase!" whispered Bernard, pointing to Medusa's half-packed luggage.

Without noticing the two mice, Medusa threw the suitcase into her car and set off for the airport. But she drove so fast that the suitcase bounced out of the car, with Bianca and Bernard inside!

How would they get to Devil's Bayou now? Then Bianca had an idea. The pair made their way to a building with a sign reading 'Albatross Airlines'.

A large albatross offered to fly them to Devil's Bayou.

Bianca and Bernard took their seats and prepared for take-off. But Bernard was not very happy: he didn't like the idea of flying at all!

Weaving his way skilfully around the skyscrapers, the albatross flew the pair towards Devil's Bayou. Bianca was having a wonderful time, but Bernard was more and more convinced that they would have been better off going by train!

Meanwhile, deep in the spooky wilds of Devil's Bayou, a little girl was running away from the wreck of an old riverboat, clutching a small teddy bear in her arms.

"Penny!" Medusa screeched furiously from the boat. "That little urchin has run off again!"

Medusa ordered her pet crocodiles, Brutus and Nero, to bring Penny back to her.

Medusa jumped into her swampmobile, yelling at her partner Snoops, "Send up those flares! Let's light up the whole swamp and, when you catch sight of them, let off a rocket!"

Just as the albatross was about to land in the swamp, he was dazzled by the flares that Snoops had set off. The two mice were thrown out of their seats! But Bernard used his umbrella as a parachute and they landed safely. Waiting for them on the ground were Ellie Mae and her husband Luke.

Suddenly, from the depths of the swamp, Brutus and Nero appeared, carrying Penny and her teddy.

"Oh, no!" cried Bianca. "Quick, we must find out where they're taking her."

"You'll need a boat," said Ellie Mae. "Evinrude owns the fastest boat in the bayou."

Evinrude was
a dragonfly. His
boat was a leaf,
which he propelled
by flapping his
strong wings.
Evinrude took
Bianca and Bernard
across the dark waters
of the swamp, keeping
the two crocodiles in sight.
    "Faster, Evinrude, faster!"
shouted Bianca anxiously.

At last Evinrude reached the wreck.
Bianca and Bernard listened in on what Medusa
was saying to little Penny.

"You know what would make your dear Auntie Medusa really happy?" Medusa asked sweetly.

"Yes," the little girl replied. "You want me to find that diamond. But I have tried so hard to find it, I really have!"

"I know you've tried, but you must try harder!" replied the evil Medusa, as Snoops gave Penny a menacing look.

Unfortunately, it wasn't long before Brutus and
Nero discovered Bianca and Bernard's hiding place.
"Oops, Miss Bianca, they can smell your per-per-
perfume!" Bernard stammered.

The mice made a run for it but the two crocodiles followed hot on their heels. Finally, after a long chase, the mice gave the creepy crocs the slip and reached Penny's room.

Penny was kneeling by her bed, saying her prayers. She prayed for her teddy and for all the other children at the orphanage. Then she prayed that her S.O.S. message would be found, because she knew she couldn't escape without help.

Poor Penny burst into tears.

"Penny, my dear, don't cry. We're here to help you," Miss Bianca reassured her.

"Where did you come from?" asked the startled girl.

"We found your message," explained Bernard, "and we've come to rescue you." Little Penny was puzzled: "Didn't you bring the police with you?" she asked.

"No," replied Bernard, "we're on our own!" "But," continued Bianca, "if the three of us work together and we have a little faith..."

"... faith makes everything possible," finished Penny.

So the three of them hatched a plan to foil Medusa. They would need help, so Bernard asked Evinrude to round up all his friends in the swamp.

The next morning Medusa and Snoops collected
Penny from her room. They took her to the Black
Hole, which was a cave with an opening so narrow
that only a child could squeeze through it. But at
least Penny wasn't alone; Bianca and Bernard were
hiding in her pocket.

Medusa wanted to be
sure that Penny would
try her hardest to find
the jewel. She snatched
Penny's teddy bear
from her, screeching,
"Get down there and
find that big diamond,
or you'll never see your
teddy bear again!"

Penny was lowered to the floor of the cold dark cave. Bianca and Bernard crept out of her pocket.

"This was a pirates' cave," said Penny. "They used to hide their stolen jewels here. Medusa wants me to get her the Devil's Eye diamond, but no matter how hard I look, I just can't find it."

Suddenly the mice spotted a strange glimmer coming from inside a skull!

Bianca and Bernard climbed into the skull.
"Wow!" exclaimed Bernard.
"It's the Devil's Eye!" Bianca cried. "We've found it
at last!"
Penny called to Medusa that they had the
diamond. Medusa excitedly ordered them to bring it
up to her right away.

But the skull was stuck fast in the ground and
the diamond was too big to come out through the
eye sockets. The water level in the cave was rising –
there was no time to lose!

Bernard had an idea. He told Penny to use a
discarded cutlass to prise the skull apart. It worked!
Penny grabbed the diamond. Everyone jumped into the
bucket, ready to be winched back to the surface.

As soon as Penny appeared, Medusa snatched the diamond out of her hands.

"At last the Devil's Eye is mine!" she crowed in triumph. "Half of it is mine, actually!" Snoops reminded her. But Medusa had no intention of sharing her prize and the two started to quarrel, while Penny yelled, "Give me back my teddy now! You promised! It's mine!"

But Medusa replied that she was taking the bear with her. "I've grown rather fond of it!" she leered as she walked off.

Snoops chased after Medusa, determined not to let her get away with the diamond.

Meanwhile, the animals of the bayou, led by Evinrude, were rushing to board the old wreck.

First of all, Bianca and Bernard put their plan to get rid of the crocodiles in action.

Inside the wreck there was an old lift with a metal cage. Miss Bianca sprayed a little of her perfume inside it. She knew the scent would attract Brutus and Nero.

"Now!" Bernard shouted as soon as the crocodiles got into the lift. The bayou's animals slammed the lift door shut, trapping the two beasts inside!

Now for Medusa! The animals grabbed Snoops'
fireworks and, when Luke gave the signal, launched
a barrage of rockets towards Medusa. Medusa tried
to defend herself, but she backed into a rope that
Bernard had tied across the doorway. As she fell,
Medusa dropped Penny's teddy, which had the
diamond hidden inside it!

Penny snatched back her beloved teddy and started the engine of Medusa's swampmobile. They all sped away to safety as the old wreck was blown to smithereens.

Medusa wanted to go after Penny and her friends,
but her pet crocodiles had other ideas. They snapped
at her with their great gaping jaws and she had to
climb the mast of the wreck to escape. Snoops rowed
off to safety on a makeshift raft. Evil Medusa had lost
her precious diamond forever!

A few days later, Bianca and Bernard were back at the Rescue Aid Society office. Everyone was gathered round the TV and when Penny appeared on the screen, a huge cheer went up. The brave little girl had been adopted and at last she had kind parents to love her. As for the diamond, it had been donated to the museum, so that everyone could go and admire it.

But there was one more surprise to come: looking into the camera, Penny thanked the two brave little mice that had come to her rescue.

When they heard Penny's message, all the
Society's members started clapping wildly.
   Bianca, who was already planning her next
adventure, planted a kiss on Bernard's cheek,
making him blush.
   "We make a great team!" said Bernard.